ANOTHER PURPLE CRAYON ADVENTURE

HAROLD'S
ABC

STORY AND PICTURES

by
Crockett
Johnson

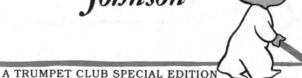

A TRUMPET CLUB SPECIAL EDITION

Published by The Trumpet Club, 666 Fifth Avenue, New York, New York 10103
Copyright © 1963 by Crockett Johnson. All rights reserved.
ISBN: 0-440-84413-4
This edition published by arrangement with HarperCollins
Children's Books, a division of HarperCollins Publishers,
New York, New York.
Printed in the United States of America   September 1991
SEM   10 9 8 7 6 5 4 3 2 1

Harold decided one evening to take a trip
through the alphabet, from A to Z.

To go on any kind of trip he had to leave
home. He started with A for Attic.

And he left his yard, taking his purple
crayon and the moon along.

To get very far he was going to need a lot of words. B is for Books.

He could find plenty of words in a pile of
big books. He was ready for anything.

Harold was always ready for something to eat. And C is for Cake.

He took a large cut of cake and ate it as
he continued on his way.

The cake made him thirsty, and he wanted
a drink. Luckily D is for Drink.

He drank right out of the dipper. He was
eager to get on with his excursion.

He visited an enormous edifice, the tallest
building in the world.

It went up and up and up, floor after floor,
etcetera, etcetera.   E is for Etcetera.

Elevators take people up and down in big
buildings, but Harold didn't like them.

They made his stomach feel funny. He went
up, over a hundred stories, in his own way.

At the very top Harold was surprised to
see something higher than he was.

It was only the next letter of the alphabet,
flying from the roof. F is for Flag.

Now he had to get down. G is for Giant.
One happened to be passing by.

Giants generally aren't so genial. But this one grinned when Harold landed on him.

Harold explained he was in a hurry. The
giant gently set him on the ground.

He hastened along. H is for Horse. One
way to go fast is on horseback.

Unfortunately the horse didn't turn out to look much like a real horse.

It made a rather good hobby horse, but a hobby horse doesn't go anywhere.

Harold had to think of some other way to
speed his trip. I is for Idea.

He went to work on the next letter with his purple crayon. J is for Jet.

In a jiffy he had a speedy little jet plane
ready to take off.

Harold hopped into it and rocketed away.
It overtook the next letter in no time.

Harold jumped out and grabbed on, think-
ing hard of a word for it.

K is for Kite, flying on a string. Harold began to climb down the string.

Suddenly a quicker way of getting down
struck Harold.

L is for Lightning. Harold held tight to
the purple crayon, going like a streak.

He landed on a pair of tall peaks, high and lonely. M is for Mountain.

He looked for somebody to ask where these
mountains were.   N is for Nobody.

Off in the sky he saw an orbiting object.
It looked like a strange planet.

O is for Ours. Our earth! The mountains
were on the rim of the moon.

He looked over the edge, at the side of
the moon he had never seen.

Down below him was the next letter of the
alphabet. Taking aim, he jumped.

P

P is for Parachute, he said as he plunged
to a plain on the far side of the moon.

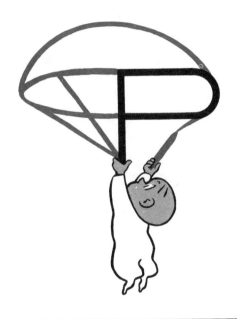

And suddenly he wondered how he could
get back over the ridge of mountains.

He would have to ask the man in the moon,
or the king, or whoever was in charge.

Q is for Queen.   She was Urania, queen of
the sky, she told Harold, who bowed.

Only **King Uranus** could help Harold get home, she said, but the king was away.

Far away, the queen said, across land and
sea. Harold decided to ride there.

R is for Rhinoceros, roaming both land and water.   But it was a slow rough ride.

S

And when Harold reached the sea, and the
next letter, he had a better idea.

S is for Sea Serpent. Harold sailed across
the moon ocean at a smooth swift speed.

He landed far away, looking for the king of
the sky who was supposed to be there.

T is for Telescope. He set it up on a tripod.
All he saw through it was another letter.

The queen had mentioned the king's name.
Harold remembered it. U is for Uranus.

He drew the king's attention and asked how
to get back across the moon mountains.

King Uranus in his ermine robe stood silent
and majestic, considering the question.

Then, with a kingly gesture, he waved Harold
forward and onward.

Harold trudged along toward another letter,
away off in the distance.

It was V for Valley. He could go through it
to the side of the moon near the earth.

Four more letters and he would be through
the whole alphabet.

But the biggest letter of all barred his way.
He tried to think of a word for it, quickly.

W is for Witch, wicked and waiting. And it
looked as if he would never get through.

Harold nearly gave up. But then he saw the
next letter, right near by.

X is for Xxxing-Out.   Harold had had to X
things out before, lots of times.

It worked this time too. Witches are very
susceptible to such treatment.

He had made so many marks it was hard to
get through them, but Harold managed.

Magically he found himself in a familiar
garden, with the moon high in the sky.

Y is for Yard, his own yard.   He was home!
And there was one letter left.

In his bedroom, as he dozed off, he made up a word. Z is for Zzzl, or little snore.